J
ELEM
Abbott

EAST GRANBY PUBLIC LIBRARY

The knights of Silversnow.

3328000054645/

8/03
re Q

P9-CBC-131

THE SECRETS OF DROON

The Knights of Silversnow

by Tony Abbott
Illustrated by Tim Jessell

A
LITTLE APPLE
PAPERBACK

SCHOLASTIC INC.
New York Toronto London Auckland Sydney
Mexico City New Delhi Hong Kong Buenos Aires

For Dolores –
each day is more
magical than the last

Book design by Dawn Adelman

If you purchased this book without a cover, you should be aware that
this book is stolen property. It was reported as "unsold and destroyed"
to the publisher, and neither the author nor the publisher has received
any payment for this "stripped book."

No part of this publication may be reproduced in whole or in part,
or stored in a retrieval system, or transmitted in any form or by any means,
electronic, mechanical, photocopying, recording, or otherwise,
without written permission of the publisher.
For information regarding permission, write to Scholastic Inc.,
Attention: Permissions Department, 557 Broadway, New York, NY 10012.

ISBN 0-439-30609-4

Text copyright © 2002 by Robert T. Abbott
Illustrations copyright © 2002 by Scholastic Inc.

All rights reserved. Published by Scholastic Inc.
SCHOLASTIC, LITTLE APPLE PAPERBACKS, and associated logos
are trademarks and/or registered trademarks of Scholastic Inc.

12 11 10 9 8 7 6 5   3 4 5 6 7/0

Printed in the U.S.A.   40
First Scholastic printing, August 2002

Contents

One

Turvy-Topsy

"I'm going to use it. I can't use it. Yes I will! No I won't. Here I go. I better not. I'm using it!"

"I definitely agree."

Eric Hinkle and Neal Kroger were pacing back and forth across their friend Julie Rubin's front yard. A large FOR SALE sign was sticking out of the lawn next to them. Julie's father had gotten a new job and Julie was moving away — that very day.

But it wasn't the sign that the two boys were talking about. It was the object in Eric's hand. It had a narrow golden shaft about a foot long with a glowing purple flower at its tip. It was a magical object called the Wand of Urik.

And it came from Droon.

"I still can't believe you found the wand," said Neal, wanting to touch the wand but not daring to. "It was lost in Droon forever and here you go and find it just like that!"

Droon was the strange and mysterious world Eric and his friends had discovered under his basement. Since the first time they had descended the rainbow-colored stairs, Droon had filled their lives with wonder, adventure, and danger.

And friends, too. That was the best part.

Their closest friend in Droon was a young wizard named Princess Keeah.

Together with Galen Longbeard, the old first wizard of Droon, and Max, his spider troll helper, and many other friendly folks, Eric, Neal, and Julie had helped the princess keep Droon free from the clutches of a wicked sorcerer named Lord Sparr.

Right now, Sparr was riding a huge fiery snake through the old underworld of Goll. Galen was following Sparr, trying to stop the sorcerer's latest evil plan. Whatever that was.

"The wand really found me," said Eric, stopping to stare at the wand. "It was disguised as an old stick. I can't believe I kept throwing it away, but it kept finding me again!"

Neal peered closely at the wand's

bright flower. "Probably because you're sort of a wizard."

Eric smiled at that. He was sort of a wizard.

Ever since he had been struck by a blast of Princess Keeah's magic, he had been able to do strange things.

He could make powerful blue light shoot from his fingertips. He could speak to his friends just using his thoughts. And he had visions of things that hadn't happened yet.

Eric looked at Julie's front door. It was open.

"Maybe I'm supposed to have the wand," he said. "Just to keep Julie from moving away. Maybe that's why it followed me, you know?"

"But Keeah said magic is tricky," Neal said. "So maybe we shouldn't —"

Just then — *rmmm!* — a large moving

van rumbled down the street toward Julie's house.

Eric shuddered. "That's it. I can't let Julie move away. I'm doing it!"

Feeling the power of the wand surge through him, Eric marched up to Julie's front door.

Piles of boxes were stacked up just inside the door. Julie's father was removing paintings from the walls and stacking them on the sofa.

Holding the wand behind his back, Eric pulled open the screen door and walked in.

"Hi, Mr. Rubin," said Eric. "Is Julie around?"

"Hi, Eric, Neal," said Mr. Rubin with a sigh. "Forgive the mess. We have so much . . . stuff. Julie! Your friends are here!" He smiled at the kids, then carried the paintings out of the room.

A moment later, Julie came downstairs

carrying a big carton full of toys. Her cat, Pinky, was nestled right in the middle of them. Eric could see that Julie's eyes were red. She'd been crying.

"Hi, guys," she said. "I have so many baby toys I haven't seen for years. They make me remember all kinds of stuff."

Eric checked to see that they were alone, then, grinning, he brought the wand around for Julie to see. The flower at its tip was glowing brightly.

Julie stared at it. "Oh, my gosh. Is that —"

"Yes!" Neal blurted out. "The Wand of Urik! It followed Eric up from Droon! Now we have it!"

Julie's eyes widened. "Do you think it could . . . No, Keeah warned us . . . I mean, that wand *created* the rainbow stairs! It's got too much power to fool with. Shouldn't we bring it back?"

"We'll bring it back," said Eric. "Definitely. Just as soon as we do — this!"

Julie drew a breath. "Are you sure about this?"

"Pretty sure!" said Neal, stepping back. "At least, I think so. . . ."

With a quick flourish, Eric waved the wand over his head. Remembering the riddles Galen had spoken when he used the wand, he said, *"Staying is good. Julie is good. Julie is staying!"*

Suddenly, the wand flooded the room with quivering purple light that threw Eric sharply backward. "Whoa! That's power!" he said.

An instant later, the light faded and the room went back to normal.

"That was cool," said Neal, helping Eric up.

Julie looked around. "Okay, now what —"

Brrrng! The phone rang loudly in the kitchen. The kids could hear Mr. Rubin pick it up.

"Hello? Yes, it is. What? Really? But I thought . . . Yes. Are you sure? Okay. Tomorrow. Yes!"

He hung up the phone, then came into the living room and removed his glasses.

"Dad, what is it?" asked Julie.

"It's the most amazing thing," he said. "My old company offered me an even better job. I'm . . . I'm going to take it. Julie, we're not moving!"

Her mouth dropped open. "Dad, is this true? I mean, are you kidding? I mean — yay!"

"Yay is right!" Mr. Rubin exclaimed. "I've got to go tell your mother! Honey —"

He rushed from the room.

With a huge grin, Eric slid the wand into

his belt and folded his arms. "Yes, yes. Applause won't be necessary. Nice, but not necessary —"

Julie began jumping up and down. "Thank you, Eric! This is so great! It's greater than great! It's unbelievable! This is awesome! Pinky!"

Julie scooped her cat into her arms and twirled around. "Pinky, we're not leaving! Oh, Pinky, isn't this great?"

"Woof!" said the cat.

Julie stopped twirling. "Pinky . . . ?"

"Woof! Woooof!" The cat leaped from her arms and shot behind a stack of packing boxes.

Neal squinted at the cat. "Has Pinky been eating dog food by mistake?"

"Uh-oh. . . ." Eric stared at the wand in his belt. The gleaming flower at its tip dulled for a second. Then one of the purple petals shriveled and fell, vanishing before it hit the carpet.

He looked up. Neither Julie nor Neal had seen it.

Eric trembled suddenly. "Um . . . I think we'd better get to Droon right away —"

He headed to the door, then stopped short, his friends bumping into him from behind.

"Holy cow," said Neal. "Who are *they*?"

The moving van was nowhere in sight. Instead, a procession of figures in long, hooded cloaks was marching slowly up the street. They kept chanting, *"Om — yee — Pesh! Peshhhhh!"*

Julie shook her head. "Those guys are not from around here. *Pesh*? That's not even a word —"

"And those aren't even guys," said Neal. "Look!"

A green tail flicked up behind one of

the hooded figures as it tossed a dark ball into the air. The ball rose high, then made a sudden crackling noise.

An instant later, a sleek flying lizard appeared in the sky over them. It had several sets of wings along its back and many legs beneath it. It coiled in the air and made a loud hissing sound.

"This is not supposed to happen," said Neal.

Eric shook his head. "It's because of the wand. I shouldn't have used it."

A moment later — *poomf!* — the lizard was gone. The hooded creatures were gone. The children stood alone in Julie's front yard.

Julie turned. "Guys, I think we'd better —"

"I think so, too!" said Neal.

The three friends dashed across the street to Eric's house. Bursting into the kitchen, they found — *blam! clonk! slam!* —

the kitchen cabinets banging open and shut, and the pots and pans clanging and clattering off the shelves.

Neal dodged a flying saucepan. "Yikes! Things are sure getting turvy-topsy around here!"

"Don't you mean *topsy-turvy*?" asked Julie.

Neal laughed. "Sure, on a normal day!"

"Gang, let's go!" said Eric. "Now!"

In a flash, they were down the basement stairs and heading straight for the closet underneath.

Opening the closet door, Julie switched on the ceiling light, and the kids piled in. Eric closed the door and turned off the light. *Click*.

The closet went dark, then — *whoosh!* — a staircase stood curving down from the house, shimmering in every color of the rainbow.

"The wand created these stairs ages ago," said Eric. "I shouldn't have used it."

Julie turned to him. "We all wanted to use it. So, okay, Pinky barked and we saw a flying lizard. I'm still glad you used it to keep me here."

"That was the easy part," he replied. "The hard part will be fixing things —"

Clang! Blam! Pans were still flying upstairs.

"And cleaning up!" said Neal. "Let's go!"

Sticking close together, the three friends descended the stairs. Just as the rainbow light began to fade, they spotted a yellow circle of light.

It was the outline of a small round door.

"Should we knock?" asked Neal.

"Let's be careful and just peek in," said Julie.

Eric stepped off the stairs and quietly opened the door. Beyond it was a room cheerily decorated with a small bed and pink walls. "Hey, it looks like Keeah's room in Jaffa City —"

Suddenly, the far door burst open and Princess Keeah dashed in, bolting the door behind her. Her golden hair was a mess, her clothes torn and dirty, her eyes wild.

"Keeah?" said Eric. "Is everything okay?"

She whirled around. "No! Here they come!"

Julie blinked. "Here *who* come —"

"The marmets!"

Blam! The far door blasted open and a horde of furry little orange creatures leaped in. They were squealing and yelping and shouting and crying a single word.

"CHEEEEEEESE!"

Two

Pesty Pests!

"They're all over the palace," cried Keeah. "Help me catch them!"

But already the fuzzy marmets were everywhere. They swung from the ceiling lights and hung from the bedposts. They crawled over the windowsill and scurried under the chair.

"Cheeeeeese!" snarled one marmet, leaping onto Keeah's bookshelf.

"Get off there!" Keeah snapped, grabbing a broom and whisking the marmet away.

As Eric jumped to join her, Keeah saw the wand hanging from his belt. "Eric, is that —"

He grinned at her. "Yes, the Wand of Urik! It sort of followed me to my house."

"I can't believe you found it!"

"Found it," said Neal. "And used it. And —"

"Woo-hoo!" came a booming laugh.

King Zello, a huge Viking of a man, came bouncing in, practically filling the room with his hugeness. "Get these pesky varmints off me!"

Two marmets dangled from his helmet.

Laughing, Neal grabbed one marmet in each hand. They turned to him, stuck out their tongues, and licked his face.

"Yuck!" he cried, letting them go.

"Tricked you!" said one marmet, scurrying away. "Now to find some cheese!"

Queen Relna, Keeah's mother, dashed in with Max, the spider troll. Max carried a large sack with his two front legs.

The queen nabbed three creatures and tossed them over her head, where Max caught them in his sack. "So much for you!" she shouted.

"Where did the marmets come from?" asked Eric, grabbing one that dropped from the ceiling.

"From there!" said Max, pointing out the window. In the center of the palace courtyard, where a fountain usually ran with sweet, cool water, there was now a rocky, earthen hole. A steady stream of marmets was pouring from the hole.

"An earthquake rumbled through here early this morning," King Zello said, tossing three chittering marmets into the sack. "The whole countryside's been hit."

Max jumped to the ceiling light and swatted two large marmets to the floor. "We've been so busy, we haven't had a chance to find out why!"

"Cheese! Cheese! We won't leave until we get some!" cried the marmets as more poured in.

Suddenly, a man in a blue robe bounded in backward, shouting, "If only there were some marmets around here!"

"Nelag!" said Julie. "Please help us!"

Nelag was the mixed-up look-alike that Galen had conjured to take his place while he was chasing Sparr in the underworld.

"Wake me when they come!" said Nelag brightly. Then he sat in a chair and fell asleep.

"Oh, this is ridiculous!" the queen said finally, jumping on the bed. "Keeah, Max, go with your friends to the Farne Woods. Find dear old Portentia. Ask her about these earthquakes. Find out when Galen is coming back. And ask her what to do about these marmets!"

Portentia was a truth teller who lived in a rock. The children had sought her advice once before.

"People, let's go!" said Keeah. Using her broom to make a path through the squealing marmets, the princess led her friends through the palace to the royal stables.

As they raced across the courtyard, the ground rumbled again, sending more marmets leaping up from the ground.

"Oh, dear, dear!" chittered Max, scampering alongside Keeah. "I fear for our poor Droon if these earthquakes continue!"

Julie looked at Eric. "I hope this isn't going on back home," she said.

"What do you mean?" asked the princess

as they entered the stable. "Is something strange happening in the Upper World, too?"

The children looked at one another.

"Only if you think a flying lizard is strange," said Neal. "Because we saw one. A big one. And crazy guys in hoods who said nutty words."

Keeah hitched up Galen's six-legged pilka, Leep, then stopped. "Is this true?" she asked. "Eric?"

Eric felt his heart race suddenly. "I used the wand to keep Julie from moving. And it worked! It worked unbelievably great! Then . . . stuff started to happen."

"Julie's cat started barking," said Neal.

"I didn't know what to do, but I had to do something," said Eric, glancing at the wand again. "I guess I shouldn't have used it."

The princess hitched up a pilka for each of them. "I might have done the same thing. But what you saw — the creatures, the flying lizard — appeared because you changed the normal course of events."

"And how do I fix that?" asked Eric.

Keeah shrugged. "I don't know what it means, but Galen once said he went back to the time before a thing happened to make it not happen."

Eric frowned. "The time before a thing happens? Now you're giving me a headache. Maybe you'd better keep the wand."

Pulling it from his belt, he handed it to her.

Fwoot! It shot right back into his hand.

"Whoa!" he gasped. "Sorry. Here."

Fwoot! It returned to him again.

Keeah frowned. "The wand has some kind of possession spell on it. We'll ask Galen about it when we find him —"

"*If* we find him!" said Max. "Please hurry."

Eric swallowed hard. "Keeah, let's stick close on this trip. I don't want to get into more trouble with the wand."

The princess returned his smile. "It's a deal. Now, everybody, take your reins and snap them once. We're on our way to see Portentia!"

The kids mounted the pilkas. With a quick snap of leather, the shaggy camel-like creatures dashed to the city gates.

"Hurry!" King Zello shouted from Keeah's window as he pulled two squirming marmets from underneath his armor. "I'm . . . ticklish!"

Waving to her giggling father, Keeah turned Leep away from the city.

Another quake rumbled beneath them as the small group galloped straight for the dark green fullness of the Farne Woods.

Three

Riddles in the Woods

Minutes later, the small band entered the forest. The towering pines near the outer edge soon gave way to gnarled oaks whose thick, drooping branches hung with vines.

"I love these woods," said Keeah, slowing her pilka to a trot on the twisting paths. "They go back to the very beginning of Droon."

"When my master was just a boy," said Max.

"My mother wants me to start keeping a diary of everything that happens," said the princess, patting a pouch on her belt. "I've got my notebook here. Maybe someday it'll be in Galen's library."

"I love our library at home," said Julie. "I'm glad I don't have to leave it behind. Very glad."

Eric was happy for Julie. But he felt nervous and angry with himself. While they rode along the shadowy paths, he couldn't get his mind off what might be going on back in the Upper World. And he kept seeing the wand's purple petal fall off and disappear.

He wondered why he hadn't told anyone about the petals.

Later, when I understand it more, I'll tell Keeah, he thought. *No, now. I'd better do it now.*

Pulling his pilka alongside the princess, he said, "Um, Keeah —"

Suddenly, a blinding flash of light burst behind his eyes. "Whoa!" He slid off his pilka and tumbled to the ground.

"Way to ride, cowboy," said Neal, turning to him. "Wait — he's having a vision! Eric, are you all right —" Neal's voice faded away.

Out of the blinding light of his vision Eric saw a shape. It was the zigzag shape of a stairway leading upward. But it was not the rainbow stairs that brought them to Droon.

This stairway was made of shiny black stone. It stood on a bed of white earth and shot straight up into the clouds. The steps were covered with frost, and on each one were strange hoofprints.

"Eric, can you hear me?" said a voice.

He kept his eyes closed and tried to see if there were any other clues to what he was seeing. But the more he tried, the less clear it became. Finally, the stairs vanished.

When Eric popped his eyes open, his friends were on the ground staring at him. He told them everything he'd seen. "The stairs looked familiar, but I don't know from where."

Julie frowned. "Black stairs. We saw black stairs in the wall paintings in Ko's palace."

Eric thought back to the black stone palace of Emperer Ko, ruler of ancient Goll. It was there that they'd found the wand. "Maybe. But why —"

"WHAT'S THAT CHATTER-R-R-R!" thundered a voice from the clearing just ahead. "C-C-COME FORWARD RIGHT NOW-W-W!"

The five friends entered a small clearing

surrounded by withered trees. At the back was a large gray boulder with a hole in the middle of it. The hole was shaped like a mouth.

"WHO D-DARES D-DISTURB POR-TENTIA⸮" boomed a voice coming from the stone. With each sputtered syllable, a spray of wet pebbles scattered over the children.

Keeah brushed the pebbles from her clothes and stepped forward. "Excuse me, Portentia. It's me, Princess Keeah, and my friends —"

"I KNOW-W-W WHO Y-Y-YOU ARE!" the rock thundered. "And, boy, have I got a lot to tell you! So pull up a rock and listen!"

Eric smiled to hear the oracle's cheery voice again. Neal had once said she sounded like his grandmother, and that was true. After all she'd done, Portentia was like family to them.

The five friends drew nearer to the boulder.

"First, so I don't feel so dumb, tell me exactly why you have come," said the oracle, sprinkling a small spray of gravel.

"Earthquakes have thundered all over Droon," said Max. "They're messing up everything! The queen has sent us to find out why."

Portentia sucked in a breath. "Sparr rides a fiery snake! It causes our poor Droon to quake!"

"You mean — Kahfoo?" asked Keeah.

"Bless you," said Portentia.

Eric laughed. "No, she means Kahfoo, the snake Sparr is riding through the underworld."

"The very same," said the oracle. "And if you stop them, it'll be a treat. Because when the ground rumbles it tickles my feet!"

"Stones have feet?" Neal whispered.

"I heard that!" said Portentia with a chuckle.

"Why is Sparr in Goll?" asked Keeah.

"Well, it's not to shop at a pastry stall!" the oracle replied. "Sparr has gone away to Goll to find a weapon feared by all. His power grows, so does his might, while Galen's trapped in a cave of night."

Max jumped. "My master! In trouble? How can we help him?"

"To the Ice Hills you must go, where lies the castle of Silversnow. Asleep for years within its wall, three noble knights await your call. They fight with axes and a shield. Their bravery will never yield!"

"Silversnow!" said Keeah, reaching for her notebook. "I've heard of it. An old legend talks of the Knights of Silversnow. They are great and noble warriors who have slept for centuries, waiting for the hour when Droon needs them most."

"Yeah, well, thanks to Sparr," said Neal, "that hour is coming fast —"

"So does another earthquake blast!" snapped the oracle as the earth trembled again. "Hide, my dears! Someone's coming near!"

All of a sudden, the ground exploded in a shower of dirt and rocks. The kids dived behind Portentia, then peeped around to the clearing.

A black hole split open in the earth, and three winged creatures crawled up from the depths.

Their skin was scaly and lizardlike, but their heads had wrinkled old faces, with pointed red noses, scraggly beards, long gray hair, and teeth that were chipped and broken.

They shook out their wings, scattering mud and dirt all around.

"Haggons!" gasped Max. "Hag dragons!

Galen told me of them once. Bad, bad creatures!"

"Where to?" said the largest haggon, with a voice that squealed like a pig's.

The second one nosed the air. "The weather is turning cold. We must follow the chill air."

"I'm getting a chill," said the third, sniffling.

"Here, I'll warm you," said the first. "Ha-roooooo!" A blast of flame blossomed from the dragon's mouth and engulfed the other.

"Singed my wings, you did! Why, I'll —"

"Stop it, you two!" snarled the middle one. "Deep in Goll, Sparr continues his quest, but he told us what we must do —"

"I was there, I heard him!" snarled the second.

"So what are we waiting for?" said the third. "Fly, sisters, fly to the Ice Hills!"

"To do Sparr's nasty chores!" said the first.

With a terrible wet flapping noise, the three haggons lifted from the pit. They circled the forest once, twice, then took to the clouds.

"I guess we know where we're going," said Keeah. "To the Ice Hills, everyone!"

"Wait," said Max, bowing to the oracle one last time. "Portentia, what about the marmets? They're wrecking the palace looking for cheese!"

"Tell them where the cheese is, if you please!" she replied.

"And where is that?" asked Keeah.

"You know, Keeah, I haven't the faintest idea!" said Portentia. "But here is something else I've seen. I don't know exactly what it means. A strange and golden light, a jeweled door, leads to adventure in the time before!"

"Adventure," said Neal. "We like that."

"And jewels are cool," said Julie.

Eric frowned. "The time before? The time before what? Here comes my headache again — it's so confusing."

"Sorry it's all jumbled, it's not my choosing," said the oracle. "But now for a big thundering finish — PORTENTIA HAS SP-SP-SPOKEN — GO!"

Even before the last spray of pebbles struck the ground, the children were back on their pilkas and riding away from the grove.

As they rode, a chill wind swept into the forest. Leaves quivered and tore away from their branches. Then, just as they looked up, the children shivered to see the first snowflakes floating down through the thick trees.

Four

Scary Caravan

Across the wind-torn plains Max and the children raced, Keeah and Eric sharing the lead.

The sky above them was as gray as iron. The first scattered flakes of snow gave way to larger blotchy shapes as they rode to higher ground.

"It's definitely getting colder," said Julie, shivering and wrapping her arms around herself.

"The Ice Hills have winter all year round," said Keeah. "We're already getting closer."

"Poor me!" said Neal, clapping his hands to keep warm. "I didn't wear my blizzard clothes!"

"I can help with that," chirped Max. Stopping for but a moment, he quickly wove coats and boots for the children with his thick spider silk.

Putting them on, the kids discovered that the coats were not only lightweight and snugly, but invisible.

"Cool!" said Neal. "I mean — warm!"

Soon, they galloped away again.

After an hour, Keeah raised her hand. The children tugged their reins, stopping the pilkas at the crest of a snowy ridge.

Below them was a winding channel left by a once-deep but now dried-out river. In the distance stood five white-topped peaks of enormous height, completely covered in ice.

"The Ice Hills of Tarabat," said Keeah. "We're nearly there —"

Errrk! Errrk!

A sudden creaking sound echoed up from the riverbed below.

"What's that?" said Max. "It sounds terrible!"

"Something's coming around that curve below," said Eric. He jumped from his pilka and made his way carefully to the crest of the ridge. "Holy cow! It's Ninns. Lots of them!"

Marching along the riverbed below were hundreds of Sparr's red warriors. Tugging thick ropes behind them, they pulled a giant wagon whose misshapen wheels creaked and squealed over the dried bed of stones.

On the wagon was a tower.

It was enormous — a crazy, crooked tower, made of wooden planks and logs nailed sloppily together, teetering and wobbling as it rolled.

"It's as tall as a mountain!" said Neal.

"And getting taller all the time," said Keeah.

Using ropes dangling down from the tower's top, the Ninns were hoisting up more wood. The clatter of hammers at the summit was nearly as loud as the creaking wheels below.

"What's the tower even for?" asked Neal.

"For falling over!" snarled Max. "Look at that sloppy work. The Ninns never *could* build a proper tower!"

Keeah's eyes grew large. "I know what it's for. I've seen pictures of it in Galen's *Chronicles*. It is a war tower, to get Ninns into high places —"

"Like the Ice Hills?" asked Julie. "Do you think that's where they're going?"

"Let's find out," said Keeah with a sly grin. "Galen wrote about spying in his *Chronicles,* too. Julie, come with me. The rest of you keep going to the Ice Hills. We'll meet up after we discover the Ninns' plans."

"Don't get caught!" chittered Max nervously.

The princess laughed. "You can't catch something you don't see!" Then she whispered some words and waved her hand over herself and Julie. Julie giggled as the air whooshed all around them in a swirl of misty, pink-colored fog.

Soon the two girls were invisible.

"Julie, come on," said Keeah from within the fog. "The Ninns will never know we're there!"

The pink mist floated down the steep

side of the riverbed to the end of the Ninn caravan.

"I wonder if they have a blue fog for boys," said Neal.

Eric smiled. "Yeah, magic is very cool. Well, it is if you know what you're doing."

He glanced at the wand in his belt. Its purple flower remained dull, its petals folded.

"Let's keep going," said Max.

Taking the girls' pilkas with them, Eric, Neal, and Max rode carefully along the high, snowdrifted bank of the riverbed.

Suddenly, Max stopped. "Oh, no. Look down there!"

The riverbed made a big loop across the land below. Hidden in the curve of the bed was a small village. Tiny houses made of mud were stacked one on top of another.

"We've seen that kind of village before," said Neal. "Lumpies live there, don't they?"

"Quite right," said Max. "And the Ninns will roll that huge tower right through their village!"

Eric shuddered all the way down to his invisible boots. The Ninn caravan rolling like a slow red river across the land was bad enough. But to watch it destroy a peaceful village?

"No way," he said. "We can't let it happen."

Errrk! Errrk! The Ninns wound their way farther through the riverbed.

"What should we do?" asked Neal.

Eric shook his head. "Well, for starters, you can stop nudging me."

Neal blinked. "I'm not nudging you."

Eric turned around to see Neal standing several feet away. Then he looked at Max.

The spider troll's eyebrows went up. "Don't look at me, Master Eric. I never nudge. I tap."

"Then who — hey!" Eric looked down at the wand. Its purple flower was full and bright and it was wiggling in his belt. "What —¿"

"The Wand of Urik wants you to use it," Max said. "It wants you to save the Lumpies!"

"No way," he said. "I messed things up in my world. Besides, I promised Keeah —"

"Keeah is not here right now," said Max. "You must make your own decisions. And quickly!"

Eric pulled the wand from his belt. The purple flower was glowing fiercely now. As he clutched the wand, a strange tingling sensation flowed into his hand and up his arm.

Errrk! Eeeek! The tower rolled faster.

"Hurry, Eric," said Neal. "The Lump-ies!"

"Here goes whatever!" Eric held the wand over his head. He made the same flourishing moves he had made earlier at Julie's house.

"Ninns in river. River turns. Ninns turn!"

Eric staggered back as the wand's flower shot out a wave of trembling purple light.

"Oh, yes!" Max squeaked with delight as the light struck the earth just ahead of the Ninns.

The riverbed wobbled and twisted and jumped and dipped. Finally, it wrenched itself away from the Lumpy village, making a wide loop across the plains, leaving the tiny village unseen by the Ninns.

"You did it!" said Max, jumping up and down. "Our little pillowy friends are safe!"

"You are one awesome wizard!" said Neal.

Eric stood there, amazed at how the

wand had carried out his spell. But as he tucked the wand back into his belt, he watched in horror as another petal dropped, vanishing as it hit the ground.

He suddenly felt sick and scared. "No, no," he muttered to himself. "I'm killing it. . . ." But, as before, his friends didn't see the petal fall.

A moment later, Keeah and Julie came floating back, their pink fog dissolving around them.

"We saw everything!" said Julie. "Good job, Eric. You're really getting the hang of this magic stuff."

He nodded. "Um, yeah. Thanks."

Keeah gave him a bright smile. "You really are becoming a master at it, Eric. Too bad we can't celebrate just yet."

"Right," said Julie. "We found out the Ninns are too chubby to be good climbers."

Max frowned. "Climbers? Oh, you mean —"

"Yes, Max," said Keeah. "They're going to the Ice Hills. Just like the haggons."

"They'll use the tower to climb up the icy cliffs," added Julie.

Neal made a face. "Man! It's like, let's get every bad guy in Droon to meet at Silversnow!"

"Ah, but thanks to Eric, we slowed the Ninns down," said Max. "Wait until Galen learns of his new powers —"

Eric glanced again at the folded wand flower. "We should just hurry and find Galen. We need him more than ever."

Keeah nodded firmly. "All together, then!"

She snapped the reins and the pilkas took off as the ground beneath them trembled once more.

Five

Out of the Frosty Earth

Two hours later, amid a howling snow-storm, the children arrived at the foot of the Ice Hills of Tarabat. The ground rose steeply to the summit of the tallest peak. Its slope, even at the base, was slick with pearly white ice.

Keeah whistled softly under her breath. "It sure seems a lot steeper from up close. I think we'll have to go on foot from here."

"Everyone take supplies," said Max,

sounding very efficient. "Rope, picks, and food —"

"I'll be in charge of the food!" said Neal, pulling two leather sacks from his pilka and heaving them over his shoulder.

"Just remember," said Julie, "the food is for everybody, you know."

Neal chuckled. "I'll keep that in mind."

Keeah turned to her pilka. "Leep, return to Jaffa City. We'll find another way." Leep nodded and led the other pilkas back across the plains.

"So, we're stuck here?" asked Eric.

"Galen has always said we must have hope," Keeah replied. "I'm hoping he'll lead us home."

Moments later, the five friends were trekking up the slippery sides of the mountain. Snow whipped in from every direction at once, filling their footprints as quickly as they made them.

"Silversnow," Julie said breathlessly, climbing over a craggy rock. "It sounds so mysterious. I mean, a castle frozen at the top of the Ice Hills of Tarabat? What do you think it will look like?"

"All ice," said Neal. "Cold and frosty."

"With glittering snow everywhere," said Max.

"I know it will be beautiful," said Keeah.

Hour after hour, over jagged rocks and deep chasms, the small troop made its way to the highest of the five peaks, where the legendary castle was said to be.

Finally, the five friends reached the summit. Wind flew across the mountaintop as one by one they pulled themselves up over the last ledge. What they saw stunned them.

What they saw was . . . nothing.

"Where is Silversnow?" asked Neal,

looking around. "I see the snow, but I see no castle."

"Did we climb the wrong hill?" asked Julie.

Eric stared at what lay before them. It was a broad, flat shelf of ice surrounded by jagged outcroppings of rock. There was no castle.

"Now what —" A sudden gust of wind forced his eyes closed. *Kkkk!* Light flashed in his head. He stumbled back toward the edge. "No!"

"Eric!" Keeah leaped over and grasped his hand as he fell. Max, Julie, and Neal rushed to either side, pulling him safely back over the edge.

"Is it a vision?" asked Julie. "What is it?"

But Eric's eyes were tightly closed. The light flashed only once, yet he saw the black stairway again. This time, a woman

was coming down. She held a small bundle in her arms.

Eric recognized her from paintings on the walls of Ko's palace, where he'd found the wand.

Her name was Zara, Queen of Light.

She was the *mother* of Lord Sparr.

Eric gasped in his vision. "You?"

The woman turned to look at him.

He stepped toward her and spoke again.

Kkkk! The silvery light flared, then faded, and the vision was over. Eric opened his eyes.

"What did you see?" asked Neal.

"The black stairway from before," Eric replied. "Only this time, a woman was coming down. It was her, the Queen of Light —"

Max gasped. "It's what Portentia predicted. A golden light. That's your vision!"

Eric frowned. "The light wasn't exactly golden. . . ."

"Did she say something?" Keeah asked.

Eric shook his head. "No, I did. Then she smiled at me. Snow began falling all around us."

"What did you say?" asked Julie.

"A magic word," Eric replied. "Her name. Zara —"

At once, the mountain trembled.

Max jumped. "Another earthquake! We'll fall off the mountain!"

Before they could move, the icy rock beneath them split open and — *vooom!* — a wall of ice shot up from under the ground. It was tall and white and glistening.

Neal jumped back. "Let's get out of here!"

"No, look!" said Keeah, keeping her balance as the trembling continued. "It's not an earthquake. It's . . . it's . . . the castle of Silversnow!"

Vooom! Another icy wall shot up from below.

Vooom-vooom-vooom! A tower, an archway, a set of curving stairs, a row of columns, ramps, floors, ceilings, and walls all erupted from the icy ground of the mountain.

Before their eyes, a vast and fabulous castle was being formed.

"The castle of Silversnow!" Keeah said, her voice full of wonder and awe. "It's magnificent!"

When the last wall shuddered into place and the rumbling subsided, the giant castle stood before them, a gleaming fortress of white, a palace of frost.

"Let's . . . let's go in," said Eric.

Huddled and trembling, they all stepped into the castle.

Wind rushed into the upper windows, sending snowflakes scattering down into the great hall.

"The knights are in here somewhere," Keeah said. "We must wake them after so many years."

On the back wall of the main room was a giant door, shimmering with silvery ice.

"Is that the jeweled door Portentia talked about?" asked Julie. "The frost is like jewels."

"Maybe," said Neal. "But if that's where the knights are sacking out, I hope someone brought the key —"

"We don't need one," said Keeah. "Look."

The princess was staring down a hallway behind them. Carved above the hall was a snowflake-shaped shield crossed by two battle-axes.

"This is the sign of the Knights of

Silversnow," said Keeah. "They're this way."

"I'm afraid," said Max.

"I think we all are," said Neal.

At the end of the hallway was a room aglow with silvery light. Three large beds stood inside. On each lay a figure in full armor dusted from head to foot with frost. Their helmets, nearly as large as garbage cans, stood by their beds.

The knights didn't move.

"Are they sleeping?" asked Eric. "Or . . . you know? After all, it's been four hundred years."

Keeah took a deep breath. "There's only one way to know." Closing her eyes, she began to whisper strange words, forming the syllables on her tongue over and over.

She makes it look so easy, Eric thought as he watched her raise her arms straight up.

Then — *poom!* — blue light flowed from the tips of her fingers. It flooded over the knights.

"Knights of Silversnow — awake!" she said.

With a popping, crunching, clattering noise, ice blew off the first knight in huge chunks.

Suddenly, the figure bolted up in bed.

"Oh!" chirped Max, sliding backward into Neal, who slammed into Julie.

The knight was a huge man, with a big round face, a bulbous nose, and a craggy beard of icicles.

First one eye popped open, then the other. He blinked when he saw the kids.

Then he shook his head like a dog, sneezed twice, and said —

"Oy, what a nap!"

Six

The Sleepers Awake

When the knight swung out of bed and planted his enormous feet on the floor, the kids could see just how very big he was.

Seven feet tall and four feet wide at the shoulders, the knight brushed the high ceiling when he stood.

"Oh, but I'm stiff!" he boomed, his voice echoing throughout the castle and back again.

Keeah blinked. "You make even my dad look small!"

He grinned down at her. "Thank you, little one. Now! What brings you all here? Wait! Don't tell me! It's gizzleberry pie time! No, wait! The royal sink is plugged! No, no, you've lost your pilka! Wait, I have it! Galen's gotten himself into trouble again!"

"That's right!" said Neal. "He's in Goll and we need to get him out —"

"I knew it!" boomed the knight, his beard dropping icicles to the floor with every word. Then he laughed heartily. "By the way, my name's Old Rolf. This one here is Lunk."

He kicked the frosty bed next to him. "Hey! Sleeping Beauty! Wake up. We have visitors."

Lunk turned over but did not wake up.

Old Rolf snorted, scooped some snow

off the floor, packed it, and dropped it on the sleeping knight — *splat!*

Lunk jumped up. "Hey, who hit me?"

"I did!" Old Rolf laughed. "Wake up! We're needed to free Galen. Droon's in trouble! These kids have come for us. Wake up tiny Smee, too."

"Tiny" Smee was anything but tiny. In fact, he was so tall that his feet dangled over the edge of the large bed.

"Wakey-wakey, Smee!" said Lunk, tickling the third knight's toes. "The legend says wake up!"

Smee rolled over and fell out of bed — *thud!* When he got up, he blinked lazily at the kids. "Hi," he said, yawning and scratching his ears.

"Well, here we are!" boomed Old Rolf. "The Knights of Silversnow, at your service! Now, just what has Galen gotten himself into this time?"

"He's trapped in Goll," said Keeah. "And there are earthquakes —"

"Oooh! Don't like Goll," snarled Lunk. "Have to go through the Darky Darkness to get *there*."

"Darky Darkness?" said Neal.

"Galen was chasing Lord Sparr," added Julie.

"Ooooh! Don't like Sparr, either!" growled Lunk. "Beady little eyes, fish fins for ears. Gives me the creeps, he does!"

The castle floor trembled beneath them.

"The earthquakes are getting closer," said Eric.

"All the more reason to free Galen," said Old Rolf. "Come on, then. Let's go find him —"

"Wait a second, where's my boot?" shouted Smee, peering under his bed. "It's missing."

Neal laughed. "These guys are going to find Galen? They can't even find their clothes!"

"Finding Galen is not the only problem," said Eric. "Sparr has called his army of Ninns here."

"That's right," said Julie. "And some creepy creatures called haggons are coming —"

Smee bolted up, still bootless. "Haggons, you say! Oooh, haggons are not our friends. Haggons are our enemies. If it's haggons, then it's —"

"Battle-axes!" boomed Lunk. Then he stomped over to a large icy chest and kicked it with his enormous foot. The lid flew open, revealing two double-bladed axes with long wooden handles.

"And there's my boot!" said Smee, tugging out a boot three feet tall. He pulled it on and helped Lunk remove the axes from the chest.

Old Rolf knelt next to his own bed, fished under it, and pulled out what looked like an enormous mixing bowl. He flipped it over and buffed the frost from the front of it.

It was not a bowl. It was a large silver shield with a snowflake design on the front. "Shield of Silversnow, how good to see you again!"

"Um, that's a big shield," said Julie.

"Big?" Old Rolf chuckled deeply as he slung the shield easily over his back. "Why, it's as large as the morning moon on the pink mountains of Saleef! Now, let's party in the Darky Darkness!"

"Still not clear on what this Darky Darkness is," Neal mumbled as they tramped out.

Eric pointed to the giant door at the end

of the main hall. "Where does that big door lead to?"

Keeah nodded brightly and pulled out her diary. "Is it someplace wonderful and magical?"

Old Rolf glanced at his fellow knights, coughed once, then said, "I couldn't tell you. That door's never been opened. It's been locked forever."

"Right. Always," said Lunk.

"Al . . . ways," Smee added with a yawn.

Eric shared a look with Keeah. She narrowed her eyes at the door even as the knights led them all from the castle to the mountain summit.

"Winter in the Ice Hills!" said Old Rolf, sucking in a huge breath, then puffing out a cloud of white mist and poking holes through it with his large fingers. "Galen always liked this time of year!"

Lunk chuckled loudly. "He was frolicking about in the snow when we first found him."

Julie blinked. "You *found* Galen?"

Old Rolf raised his giant hand. "Found him myself! Poor boy was wandering in the snow just south of here. Shivering he was, all wrapped in strange clothes. He was looking for Ko's palace."

"Told him the way was long, but he wouldn't be talked out of it," said Lunk. "He came back later and got us to fight side by side with him until Goll was crushed to smithereens."

"Then we went to sleep," said Smee. "Ah . . . sleep . . ."

Keeah scribbled busily in her diary. "Did Sparr do a sleep spell on you? What happened?"

"Nothing happened!" said Old Rolf. "After Goll fell, we got tired of waiting for Galen to call."

Smee nodded lazily. "So we fell asleep. . . ."

"Those were the days," said Lunk, his eyes growing misty. "I remember Galen had a wizardy toy with him. A magic wand, a beautiful thing, all gold and shiny. Big purple flower at the top. Most powerful object we ever saw. He lost it, though. A sad day for the forces of good."

Eric felt his heart race. He pulled the wand from his belt and held it up. It began to glow.

"A goblin stole it," said Keeah, her face radiant in the purple light, "but Eric found it."

Instantly, the three knights sank to their knees.

"The Wand of Urik!" they chimed together.

Smee and Lunk were still so stiff, they had to help each other up again.

"So, Eric," said Old Rolf. "You're a wizard, too⸮"

Eric shrugged. "I guess."

"Well, then!" the knight boomed. "We've got two wizards, two clever kids, a spider troll, and three Knights of Silversnow. If ever there was a band of battlers to enter the Darky Darkness and find Galen — we are it!"

"Shall we go⸮" asked Lunk.

"I think we should go," said Smee.

Keeah looked at Eric, Julie, Neal, and Max. She nodded. "Then let's go!"

Without another word, the band of eight headed across the snowy summit of the Ice Hill and down into the Darky Darkness.

Which, true to its name, was dark.

Very, very dark.

Seven

Strange Discoveries

The way to the Darky Darkness was through a tunnel that slanted down into the mountain. Long icicles hung from the craggy ceiling.

"Galen, ho!" called Rolf at the mouth of the tunnel. The snowy floor beneath their feet crunched with every step.

As they tramped down, Eric wondered again about Goll. It was an ancient civilization lying *under* Droon. Much of it had been buried by quakes and floods after the defeat of Ko, but its cities still lay below the surface, wrecked and deserted.

"Phew!" said Max, covering his button nose with one of his furry legs. "Goll must be nearby. I can already smell it!"

Old Rolf ducked his head under a low-hanging fringe of ice. "It's not far. Galen knew that. That's why he built Silversnow. To guard against the day when Sparr would return home."

Eric's breath caught in his throat. "Wait. Sparr was *born* in Silversnow?"

"Er, well, not quite," said Old Rolf, eyeing his fellow knights. "Near here, though. Turn left!"

"Near here?" muttered Neal as they went on. "What's near Silversnow? Clouds? It's the highest point in Droon."

"This way," said Old Rolf, leading them

deeper and deeper into the caves under the castle.

"Left, then right, then left again!" called Lunk, winding his way downward.

"Wait," said Keeah. To the right was a smaller cave. "Eric, you should see this. . . ."

He joined her and looked in. "Holy cow!"

"That's not the Darky Darkness," Old Rolf said. "The double-D is up ahead. Then we find Goll."

"Just a second," said Eric.

In the cave stood chunks of heavy black stone, cleaved from the walls, cut, shaped, and polished to a finish like glass.

"Black stone," said Julie. "Just like your visions, Eric." She turned to the knights. "What is this place?"

"It's a mine," said Rolf. "At least, it used

to be. Miners would dig up and carve the stone. This is where Ko found the black stone for his palace."

"And for those black stairs!" said Eric.

"Where?" said Smee, looking all around.

"In my mind," said Eric. "I get these visions."

"I think we should be moving along," said Smee. "Galen needs us. We need Galen. Come."

Reluctantly, the kids turned back. But as they did, the wand in Eric's belt suddenly beamed its purple light over dozens of small wooden objects scattered on the floor.

"What are these?" asked Julie, stooping to pick one up. The object was shaped like a top, round and flat on one end and tapered to a point on the other. She sent it spinning across the floor —

Whirrrr-eee-ooo-eee-rrrr!

Keeah laughed. "What a silly sound!" Leaning over, she took up what appeared to be a model of a house with tiny rooms. Seated inside were several figures of chubby blue people. "I've never seen anything quite like this."

"They're toys," said Julie, picking up a little wooden bridge. On it sat a carriage with perfectly round wheels and more blue figures inside.

"Cool," said Neal. "It's so detailed!"

"Uh, we're wasting time," said Lunk, heading for the tunnel again.

Old Rolf shook his head quickly and held him back. "A moment."

"Why are there toys in this cave?" asked Eric.

Old Rolf breathed out heavily. "The Orkins," he said. "They worked in these mines."

Keeah blinked. "I never heard of Orkins."

"They were people," said Rolf. "Big, blue, happy people — with a sad story."

"Ko took the Orkins' river from them," said Lunk, "and put them to work here."

"How do you take a river?" asked Neal.

"Ko charmed it," said Lunk. "Made it come alive. Turned it into a snake. A snake of fire —"

"Kahfoo!" Julie blurted out.

"Bless you," said Smee. "Want a tissue?"

"No, the snake's name is Kahfoo," said Keeah. "We've seen him. And right now Sparr is riding him through Goll. That's what's causing all the earthquakes."

"Could be the very same beast," said Old Rolf.

"The Orkin city was beautiful," Smee added. "Boats bouncing on the water, wonderful towers reaching for the sun. It was a long time ago."

"Without its river, the poor Orkin city fell into ruin," said Lunk. "All the Orkins — their families, too — were taken underground to work in these mines. To dig black stone for Ko's palace."

Neal picked up a toy tower carved of wood and polished until it shone like brass. Tiny colored windows were set in the wood. "This is nothing like the Ninns' junky tower."

"What happened to the Orkins?" asked Julie.

"The Ninns appeared and the Orkins vanished," said Lunk. "It was so long ago, no one remembers how it happened —"

Black dust shook down from the walls.

"Enough talk," said Old Rolf. "We must keep going." He gently pulled the children from the entrance to the mine. "Galen must be found."

Speeding around twists and turns, the knights led them deeper through the tunnels. Finally, Old Rolf stopped. Before them was a wide, dark opening, slanting down into the earth.

"Let me guess," said Julie. "The Darky Darkness?"

Lunk nodded. "Uh-huh. Goll is down there."

Neal's eyes bulged. "How far *down there?*"

"A mile. Maybe two," said Smee. "Ready?"

Neal jumped back. "But how . . . I mean, you don't expect us to just . . . I mean . . . huh?"

Old Rolf laughed, unslung his massive shield, and plopped it on the ground facedown. "The bigger the shield, the more people it'll hold. Hop on for the ride of your life."

"Ride?" asked Neal, grinning. "I love rides!"

Everyone piled into the shield. When Rolf gave the signal, Lunk and Smee gave it a running push toward the opening, then hopped on.

"Wheeeeeee!" yodeled Old Rolf. "We haven't done this since the Goll wars four hundred years ago!"

Fwish! Kkkk! Shooosh! They shot down into the Darky Darkness, coiling through steep turns, twisting and turning and nearly flipping over.

The kids squealed and shrieked. Max clutched Neal and Keeah tightly, while Julie and Eric kept each other from flying off.

Faster and faster, wilder and wilder, the shield shot this way and that through the dark.

"I'm — getting — sick!" Neal groaned.

"Just wait!" shouted Rolf. "It gets better!"

Ahead was a giant wall of black stone.

Julie gasped. "Oh, no! We're not —"

"Oh, yes, we are!"

Wha-boom! The shield slammed into the wall and burst through it, bouncing and sliding and scraping across rough stone until Lunk and Smee stuck their feet out and stopped the shield.

"Gosh!" murmured Old Rolf, looking around.

They had entered the crumbled ruins of Goll.

And right there, not ten yards away, trapped up to his frost-white beard in a mound of green glop, was Galen Longbeard, first wizard of Droon.

Eight

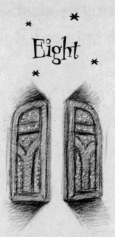

A Big, Big Secret

"My poor master," chirped Max, scampering over to the old wizard. "You've been slimed!"

"Dear friends!" cried Galen, a huge smile on his face. "I was hoping you would come!"

Galen was nearly covered in green oozy goo. It was thick, sticky, and it smelled very bad.

"Ha!" Old Rolf laughed, slapping Lunk

on the arm. "Look at our old friend, boys! His beard's a bit longer and whiter, but he's still messing up his spells! Well, well, after all these years!"

Galen narrowed his eyes at his old companions. "Yes, well, you could help get me out!"

"How did you get so tangled up¿" asked Keeah, a smile creeping over her face.

The wizard groaned. "You see, I was trying a spell to steal Ko's magic sword from Sparr, and at the very second I did the spell, well, that snake of his — Kahfoo — *spat* at me!"

"Ha! That's the problem with Goll, isn't it¿" said Lunk. "The Dark Realm and all that. Good spells just go *pfft!*"

Old Rolf was still quaking with laughter. "We'd better get the old fellow out before the goop hardens. Otherwise, he'll be stuck here forever!"

While Lunk and Smee unleashed their axes on the hardening slime, the wizard spotted the wand in Eric's belt. His forehead wrinkled slowly. Suddenly, his old dry eyes were moist.

"So, Eric, you found it, after all this time."

Eric nodded, removing the wand from his belt.

"We found the Moon Scroll," he said. "That's how we located Ko's palace. Here, it's yours."

The moment one of Galen's arms was free, he reached for the wand.

Fwoot! As before, it shot right back to Eric.

"Oh, man! I'm sorry," he said. "Here —"

"No." The wizard shook his head, smiling. "You hold it for me. I have a feeling it likes being where it is, at least for now. Besides — oh, dear!"

"What is it?" chirped Max.

Galen pointed with his one free hand at a ruined wall across the cavern. A band of grunting Ninn warriors stomped out from behind it.

"Them not escape!" one Ninn growled.

Neal groaned. "Can't Ninns *ever* lighten up?"

"Keep working, knights," said Keeah. "We'll handle them. Eric, Julie, Neal — come with me!"

The biggest Ninn, who wore a thick belt of green fur, grunted happily and started whirling a giant club over his head. "Ninns, charge!"

"Eric, double wizard blast — if we can!" said Keeah. The two wizards linked arms.

Zzz . . . zzz . . . pfft! A pale blue stream of light drifted toward the Ninns, then vanished.

"Spell no good!" said the Ninn with the club.

But Julie and Neal ran at him from the side, knocking him into two other Ninns. When he fell — *clack* — something slipped out of his belt and spun across the rough stone of the cavern, all the way over to Eric and Keeah.

Whirrrr-eee-ooo-eee-rrrr!

"Gimme!" yelled the Ninn, rushing at them.

Eric gasped. "It's a toy! An Orkin toy!"

The Ninn stopped and looked at Eric.

"Or-kin?" he grunted. A quizzical expression shot across his face from his thick red brow to his pointy red chin. "Orkin?"

Keeah nodded. "You found this in the mine!"

"Mine? No! It *mine*!" The Ninn pushed Eric and Keeah aside and closed his giant six-fingered claw around the spinning top.

Kla-bam! Galen finally burst free of the goop. The Ninns took one look at the wizard storming at them and dashed out the way they had come.

Eric turned to Keeah. "Did you see the way he looked at us? It was weird."

"It's almost as if he remembered the Orkins," said Keeah. "It's like he knew the name. . . ."

Galen headed back to the busted doorway. "The Ninns will warn Sparr that we are here and that I am free. He will act quickly —"

The mountain trembled around them.

"And we must act quickly to defend Silversnow!" said Old Rolf, scooping up his giant shield.

Eric turned to face the knight. "Defend Silversnow? Why?"

Old Rolf shot a look at Galen. The wizard nodded.

Julie gasped. "Wait a second. The big door! You said Galen built Silversnow to keep Sparr from going home. There's something behind the door. Something we need to protect, isn't there?"

Galen breathed out deeply. "Yes," he said. "It is what Sparr has been seeking for a long time. It is ancient and terrible. It is . . . the Dark Stair."

Eric's mind reeled. "The Dark Stair? Is that what I've been seeing in my visions? But if Ko built it with the stone from this mountain, and if Zara and baby Sparr came down the Stair, then where does it . . . I mean . . . what's at the top?"

"Cities," said Galen, casting his eyes slowly from Neal to Julie to Eric. "Houses. People . . . like you."

"Like us?" said Neal. "What do you mean?"

Galen said nothing. He didn't have to.

Eric knew. He searched for a way to put it all together, to say what he was thinking.

But it was almost too unbelievable.

"The Dark Stair leads . . . to our world!" said Eric. "It connects Droon and the Upper World."

Galen nodded as the mountain quaked again.

Keeah's eyes grew as wide as moons. "Then . . . Sparr was born . . . in the Upper World?"

Galen hung his head for an instant, then raised it again. "Now you know the truth about him."

Everyone stared at the old wizard.

"Zara, Queen of Light, had great power for good," he told them. "Ko heard of her. He built the stairs to the Upper World to steal her and bring her to Droon. With these knights, I defeated Ko and destroyed

Goll. Then I hid those awful stairs and created Silversnow to guard it."

Old Rolf scratched his beard. "But now Sparr has Ko's magic sword. And it can open any door."

"Try as I might, I could not keep Sparr from finding the sword," said Galen. "It was created of the most powerful old magic — magic that Sparr now has. My friends, what he may do could mean the end of both our worlds."

Eric looked at Keeah, then at his friends. "It sort of keeps getting worse, doesn't it?"

"That's why we have to stop it," Keeah said.

Galen smiled. "Then let us be about our business swiftly. Time is wasting. Stand close!"

He whirled his long blue cloak around

them all. Then with a great flourish and lots of arm waving, he mumbled strange words, and everyone began to rise — up through the Darky Darkness — and up through the icy mountain itself!

"How are you doing this?" asked Keeah, turning to the wizard. "I thought our power —"

"You thought our power was gone here?" said Galen with a sly smile. "If you think a thing, it can happen. Everyone's real power lies in their minds. For me. For you. For all of us. And now, hold tight!"

Up, up, up they went until — *ka whoom!* — they burst wildly out through a silvery peak, a sudden roaring fountain of crystals and snow and glistening frost.

"Here we are at Silversnow!" boomed Galen.

With quick strides, he pounced across the summit to the bottom step of the castle.

"My friends!" he said. "The time has come to free Droon of Sparr's evil ways!"

"Free Droon!" everyone cheered. "Free Droon — forever!"

But even before the echo of their words died, the snowy air was filled with the harsh flapping of wings and shrieking. "Har-har-rrr-rrr-ooo!"

Max jumped. "That sounds like — haggons!"

And there they were — the three terrible hag sisters. They shrieked once more, circled the castle, then dived.

Nine

The Battle of Battles?

As the haggons dived, Old Rolf planted his big feet on the castle steps. "Knights of Silversnow, in position! Haggons are our specialty!"

Lunk and Smee quickly turned, unslung their giant axes, and began tossing them to each other.

Fwish-fwish! Sling-sling! Fwap-fwap!

The silvery blades flashed and twinkled to and fro across the castle steps.

Julie blinked. "They're, um, juggling!"

"I love juggling," said Neal. "Cool!"

"Sisters, don't look!" shrieked the largest haggon. "Those silly old knights are trying to trick us! Sparr has sent us to conquer them! Don't look!"

But the flash and twirl of the shiny blades caught the haggons' dim eyes. They hovered above the knights, their wings fluttering slowly.

"And now for me!" Old Rolf boomed. He pulled his giant snowflake shield around, and with one powerful stroke he set the shield spinning.

Whoo-oo-oo-oosh! The silver shield spun around and around in a hypnotizing motion.

If the three flying sisters were entranced by the juggling axes, now their eyes were spinning as they followed Old Rolf's twirling silver snowflake.

"You knights are awesome —" said Eric.

"But *they* are not!" boomed Galen, pointing to a flash of red against the white castle walls. "Ninns! Let Max and our noble knights deal with the haggons. We'll follow these red fiends!"

Staying out of sight, Galen and the children pursued the Ninns up a set of coiling stairs and out onto the roof of the castle. The snow spun and the wind howled across the jagged summit.

"I count ten Ninns altogether," whispered Keeah as they took cover behind a low wall. "Not too many. I wonder what they're up to."

"One is the same one we saw in Goll," said Eric, pointing to the Orkin toy in a Ninn's furry green belt. "He looks like the group leader."

Even as the earth gave a powerful shudder and the castle walls shook, each of the Ninns drew an arrow, lit it, and shot it up. The arrows joined overhead to form a blazing beacon.

"Why are they doing that?" asked Julie.

Then they heard it — *errrk-errrk!*

"The tower!" said Keeah. "The Ninns are signaling the tower, to show where the castle is!"

A moment later, the wobbling shape of the Ninns' crazy war tower appeared out of the whirling snow.

"There are hundreds of angry Ninns in there," said Neal. "We'll need an army to stop them —"

Eric blinked. Watching the tower approach, he suddenly recalled the toy tower in the Orkin mine. It was as sleek as the Ninn one was junky.

Remembering how the Orkins had vanished when the Ninns appeared, and seeing now the toy stuck in the Ninn's belt, Eric was seized with a strange thought. "No. It's not possible, is it?"

Galen turned. "Eric, what are you thinking?"

"Sir," said Eric, "can you slow down the tower *and* keep the castle from crumbling around us, just for a little while?"

The wizard gave him a quizzical look. "Hmm. A double delaying spell? Well, I *do* have two hands. Yes, I can do that! But you . . ."

Galen looked so deeply at Eric, it felt as if the wizard were reading his thoughts.

"I sense what you are thinking," said the wizard. "We must hope that it will work." With that, he slipped away to a corner of the roof.

Neal blinked. "What might work? Tell us."

"No time to explain," said Eric. "Keeah,

can you cook up one of those pink fogs, while I —"

Eric clutched the wand, closed his eyes, and murmured words that seemed to come magically to him.

As the wand glowed brightly in his hand, that hand began to change. And not only his hand changed. Eric grew taller. His clothes turned black and a cloak appeared around him. His face grew long, and fins sprouted behind his ears.

"Lord Sparr!" Julie hissed. "Yikes! Eric, I hope that's still you under there —"

Eric chuckled. "Hey, I don't like it, either, but we need to stop the Ninns somehow, and I have a plan. It's crazy, but as Galen said — we have to have hope. And I've got plenty."

"Me, too," said Neal. "I hope this works!"

Eric breathed deeply and stomped out

behind the gathered Ninns. "My warriors!" he sneered, sounding almost exactly like the evil sorcerer.

The Ninns whirled around. "Master Sparr!" They bent down on their chubby red knees.

"I command you to follow me!" Eric said in a snarly voice. At once, the red warriors obeyed. They rushed by the children, whom Keeah had already surrounded in a misty pink fog.

"What that cloud¿" grunted the chief Ninn.

Eric gulped. "Uh . . . hair spray. You don't think I look this good on my own, do you¿"

"No, master. I mean, yes, master! I mean, we follow you now!" said the Ninn.

As Galen began his double spell, Eric stormed back down through the castle and across the clearing to the caves again.

Through the tunnels Eric led the Ninns and his invisible friends, until he reached the entrance to the mine. Entering, he trembled.

If this didn't work, he and his friends were in big trouble. He pulled out his wand. Then he transformed himself back into his normal shape.

Pop! His friends were suddenly visible again.

The Ninns blinked once, then jammed their way into the small room, laughing and grunting. They raised their bows and arrows.

"We get you now!" said the large Ninn.

Eric raised the wand high.

"Yes, Eric, use it!" said Julie, huddling behind him. "Do something. Turn them into —"

"I don't think I have to," said Eric quietly. Instead, he let the wand's light shine on the floor littered with the ancient Orkin toys.

"Ninns, look at these toys," he said.

The largest Ninn squinted at Eric, then glanced at the floor. His beady eyes grew wide.

"Toys," said Eric. "Remember? Like the one you have . . ."

The Ninn pulled the top from his belt, then stopped to pick up a shiny toy tower. In the light of the wand he ran his hard claws over the polished wood. Atop the tower were two tiny figures of chubby Orkins.

"Orkins . . ." the Ninn mumbled.

Suddenly, the Ninn's face twisted in a way the children had never seen before. He looked at Keeah. "You are . . . Princess of Droon. . . ."

Keeah's mouth dropped open. "Um . . . yes!"

The Ninn motioned to the diary sticking out of her pouch. "Stories . . . I remember . . . stories."

All of a sudden, the Ninn's stern features, his sharp chin, and his pointed ears began to change.

Even as the children watched, the red warrior's harsh expression dissolved into a softer face.

A rounder face.

A bluer face.

Ploink! The Ninn was no longer a Ninn. Just like the little figures on the toy tower, he was —

"An Orkin!" Julie gasped. "He's an Orkin!"

Another Ninn stepped forward and picked up the tiny carriage with blue figures inside.

Ploink! He changed, too. Then another, and another. Finally, five of the ten Ninns

stood there blue and soft and chubby and smiling.

The others drew back into the shadows. "Bad. Bad!" they said, edging away.

The first Orkin turned to them. "No, my brothers! Wait. The old stories were true. This is what we were before Ko made us work in the mine. Before Sparr made us fight for him. We *became* Ninns, but we were not *born* Ninns! Don't you remember what we were famous for?"

"What *were* you famous for?" asked Neal.

Errrk-errrk! A squealing noise echoed into the mine shaft outside.

"Tower here!" grunted one especially stout Ninn. "You blue. You not right! Tower here!" He rushed from the mine with the other Ninns who hadn't been transformed.

"The Ninns' tower is nearly here," said

Keeah. "Galen gave us our chance. Now we've got to get back to the castle — fast!"

The kids ran from the mine, up through the tunnels, and out to the summit, the five blue Orkins padding quickly after them.

When they burst out of the cave, Old Rolf and the knights were finishing tying up the haggons in a net of spider silk supplied by Max.

Galen was on the castle roof, a blue glow shimmering down from his fingertips.

But a moment later — *errrk-errrk!* — the Ninns' ramshackle wooden tower rolled right up to the tallest Ice Hill, and Galen's spell ended.

The tower swayed back and forth, then suddenly the top opened and a ramp slammed down onto the mountainside — *wump!* — sending up a huge spray of snow.

"Here they come!" yelled Galen.

"Thanks, Galen!" said Eric. "Let them come!"

Whooping loudly, a horde of red Ninns rushed out over the ramp and leaped onto the mountain, grunting and growling.

"Are we going to fight them?" asked Julie.

"Not at all," said the Orkin chief. "Allow me!"

Against that huge red army stood the five blue Orkins, weaponless, defenseless, and smiling.

The Ninns screeched to a stop. Some stepped toward the Orkins, curious. Others drew back.

The Orkin chief held up the toy top. "Remember what we were before we changed! Remember what we were in the time before!"

Eric jerked around. "The time before? Why does everyone keep saying that?"

Ploink! Ploink! Ploink! One red Ninn after another turned blue. The ranks of the blue creatures swelled, but not all the Ninns changed.

Galen came out of the castle, his eyes aglow. "Orkins! You have stopped the Ninns!"

Eric looked around. "So maybe there won't be a battle after all?"

Then the ground quaked, the earth exploded with rock and ice, and the flaming head of a giant snake thrust up through the ground, hissing wildly.

Riding on its back was the sorcerer himself. The laughing, angry, wicked Lord Sparr!

"The battle," cried Sparr, "begins — now!"

Ten

The Adventure of the Wand

Lord Sparr leaped off the snake's back, smoking and smoldering himself, but with a tight grin on his face. His eyes focused only on the castle.

"Don't you dare enter this castle!" said Keeah, backing up the front steps next to Galen.

Sparr stared at the two wizards. Right away, Eric could tell that he was different. It was as if being in Goll had made him stronger, more powerful. He gave off an eerie glow.

Sparr looked around at the haggons squirming in Max's web. "So, you've defeated the three sisters, have you?"

"We have, evil one!" Old Rolf snarled, setting his giant boot on one squawking haggon's tail.

"And my Ninns?" Sparr sneered. "They seem to have met their match."

Galen smiled. "They have met themselves! They shall not fight today."

"Oh, dear. Then it's up to me!" said Sparr. From a sheath on his back, he pulled a long, ornately decorated sword. Strange, dark symbols ran up the blade to its sparkling tip.

"Galen, you tracked me through the length and depth of Goll. But you could not stop me from discovering Ko's magic sword. Or the Dark Stair itself!"

With that, the sorcerer unleashed a storm of red lightning bolts shooting in every direction.

Blam-blam-blam!

Galen and Keeah were knocked down the steps and into the snow. Neal, Julie, and Max were thrown into a heap with Lunk and Smee.

Laughing, Sparr leaped into the castle. Everyone scrambled to their feet and raced inside. But as soon as they entered the main room, Sparr sprayed another round of lightning blasts.

One bolt hit Old Rolf squarely on his shield and knocked it out of his hands and across the room to Eric. Eric slid behind it, protected against the storm of red light.

"Sparr!" cried Galen, struggling to get up. "You shall not do this!"

"And who here will stop me?" Sparr asked. Then he took the sword and hurled it over his head. It flew across the room and — *flang!* — struck the giant door of ice.

Krrrrk! A jagged crack appeared from floor to ceiling, and the door opened.

Beyond it stood an enormous stairway, its black stone glittering with frost.

"The Dark Stair!" Julie gasped.

Eric felt a nudge at his side. He lowered his hand and the wand jumped into it.

"This stairway brought me to Droon," cried Sparr. "Now it will take me back —" He turned to see Eric in the shadows. "Back to *our* world!"

Eric felt sick. Knowing that Sparr was from the Upper World made his stomach turn. Knowing he wanted to return filled him with terror.

With every step Sparr took, lightning struck the great hall of Silversnow, scorching the white walls with streaks of black.

Sparr took a step onto the stair. "No one shall stop me from going . . . *home!*"

Sensing his moment, Eric flung himself out from behind the shield. He rushed at Sparr and slammed into him just as the sorcerer went to leap upward.

"Oooof!" Sparr groaned and fell to his knees. The lightning storm ceased for just an instant, but in that moment, Galen, Keeah, Julie, Neal, and the knights were on their feet again.

"Everyone join hands!" cried Galen.

Before Sparr could gather himself, their hands were grasping for one another. At once, Galen shouted, "Sparr, your days of terror are over!"

With that, a huge blast of blue light shot from them — from all of them equally — and surrounded Sparr.

"Agggh!" he groaned. "No — No — NOOO!"

Ka-whooom! The room was showered with blue light. The floor quaked. The walls of Silversnow shook. The great hall was suddenly aflame with swirling light and smoke.

Then everything went silent and still.

When the smoke cleared, Sparr was gone. The Dark Stair was crumbled in ruins. Chunks of black stone lay scattered across the frosted floor.

Peering into the castle, the few red Ninns who were left saw the ruined stairs.

"Sparr gone!" they grunted, then turned and hustled back into their tower.

Errk! Eeeek! It squeaked swiftly away.

"Oh, my gosh!" said Keeah, stepping forward slowly. "Can it be? Is Sparr . . . is he . . . gone?"

Galen strode over to the crumbled stairs, his eyes filled with wonder.

"Hip-hip-hooray!" boomed Old Rolf. Lunk and Smee embraced each other and jumped for joy.

All of a sudden, a huge hissing noise filled the air. Kahfoo, the fiery snake, surged into the castle hall, breathing fire and spitting venom.

Galen turned, his eyes flashing. "Oh! And as for you!" He stormed over to the snake and, like a younger man in full control of his powers, he pulled back his arm and punched the hissing snake in the jaw.

Fooom! The snake staggered back. Its large, flat head wobbled on its body. Then, as if it were in slow motion, it collapsed with a great hissing noise and tumbled down the castle steps.

Then it happened.

With Galen's single blow, Kahfoo's immense body magically and wonderfully transformed itself back into what it once was — a churning, splashing, crashing blue river!

"Oh!" gasped Julie. "Can you believe it?"

"Our river!" the Orkin chief cried out.

Running to the edge of the summit, everyone watched as the brand-new river rushed and spilled happily down the rocks to the valley below. It flowed right into the riverbed that had stood dry and empty for so many years.

The Ninn tower tipped over and became a leaky boat, floating toward the Lumpy village in the distance, which stayed safe and dry on the high banks.

"Our river has returned!" the Orkin chief cheered. "We can rebuild our city and get back to what we are famous for!"

Neal frowned. "That's right. We never did find out what Orkins are famous for."

The blue creature beamed. "Why, cheese, of course!"

"Cheese?" Keeah laughed. "Now I know where the marmets can go!"

A moment later, the snow stopped falling, and all of Droon was spread out below the mountains. It was a world of glittery white hills, deep valleys, magnificent shining cities, and forests of dark trees dusted with snow.

"My Droon," said Keeah, her eyes glistening.

"Our Droon," said Julie. She turned to Eric. "Thanks for using the wand this morning. I'm glad I can keep coming back here."

"Me, too," said Eric. Looking down, he saw the Wand of Urik glowing more brightly than ever. "Which reminds me. I left quite a mess back home. I need to talk to Galen about fixing it —"

He touched the wand. The instant he

did, he heard footsteps echo from the castle behind him.

While the knights dragged everyone to start a victory dance, Eric returned to the main hall.

He peered through the smoke rising from the ruined stairs, but saw no one.

The wand nudged him again. He touched it.

"Oh, my gosh!" he gasped.

What he saw before him were not ruined stairs, but sleek, shiny ones, rising upward.

And there, halfway up, was the sorcerer himself, leaping from step to step, fiery bolts of black lightning crashing down behind him.

"What?" Eric let go of the wand and the stairs were ruined again and smoky.

"It's a trick!" he cried. "Some kind of

spell! Everybody! Stop him! Sparr is getting away!"

Galen and the children dashed inside.

Clutching the wand, Eric sprang to the first shiny step. "Sparr tricked us. The stairs are still here! And he's going up!"

Galen went pale. "No, no, never! Follow him!"

But Galen and the others were still caught in the spell Sparr had conjured. They moved so slowly, it was as if they weren't moving at all.

Eric bounded up, the wand's purple glow forming a path through Sparr's lightning trail.

"The adventure of the wand!" Galen cried, reaching toward him. "Follow wherever it takes you, Eric! We are with you, we are with you —"

Eric felt his heart racing faster than ever before. He turned to look once more at

Keeah, Julie, and Neal. He saw everything in their faces he had hoped to find. They *were* with him.

He was doing this alone.

But they were with him.

Gasping for breath, he raced up the steps after Sparr. Faster and faster he ran.

As he neared the top, Eric spied a large jeweled door opening slowly before the sorcerer.

"The Upper World!" Eric cried.

Sparr leaped to the top step and opened the glistening door. Laughing cruelly and coldly, he bounded through the door in a flash.

"Eric! We will come for you!" yelled Keeah.

Breathlessly, Eric leaped through the door after Sparr and entered a world of strange and golden light.

About the Author

Tony Abbott is the author of more than three dozen funny novels for young readers, including the popular *Danger Guys* books and *The Weird Zone* series. Since childhood he has been drawn to stories that challenge the imagination, and, like Eric, Julie, and Neal, he often dreamed of finding doors that open to other worlds. Now that he is older — though not quite as old as Galen Longbeard — he believes he may have found some of those doors. They are called books. Tony Abbott was born in Ohio and now lives with his wife and two daughters in Connecticut.

For more information about Tony Abbott and the continuing saga of Droon, please visit *www.tonyabbottbooks.com*.